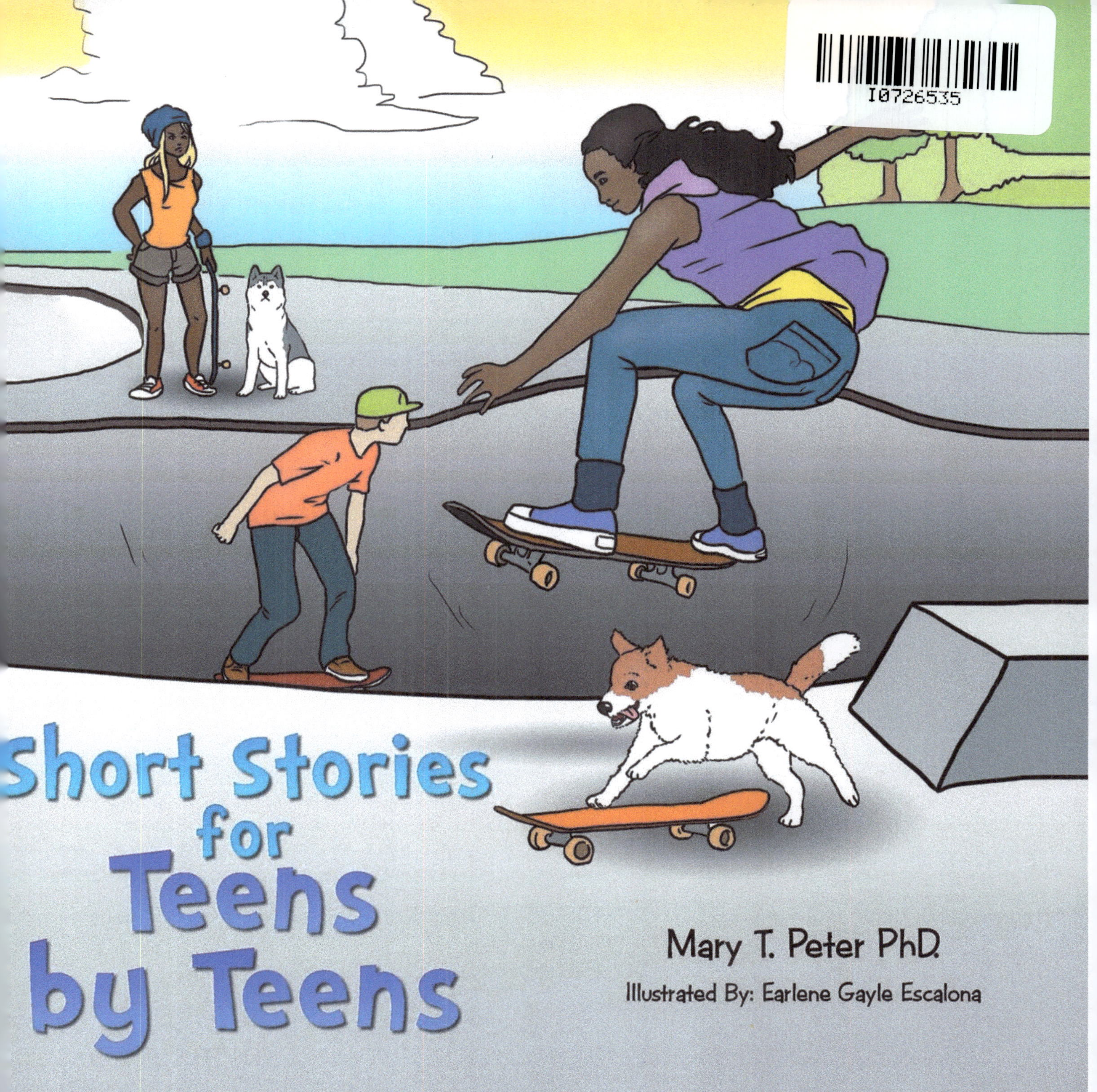

I0726535
Short Stories
for
Teens
by Teens
Mary T. Peter PhD.
Illustrated By: Earlene Gayle Escalona

Inquiries and Book Orders should be addressed to:

Great Writers Media
Email: info@greatwritersmedia.com
Phone: 877-600-5469

ISBN: 978-1-960605-56-6 (sc)
ISBN: 978-1-960605-55-9 (ebk)

What a Dream!

It was always my dream to one day publish a book with the creative thinking and dreams of the young students in my Language Arts class. In today's world of high completion for limited resources in a global society, young people need to be told that they have an opportunity to explore their creativity and goals in order to be able to participate in global completion for education and jobs. Young people are endowed with a wealth of information, thanks to technology and innovation coupled with creativity. Young people also need to know that they can capture creative skills and talents through writing. The big idea in my Language Arts class is that students will be able to process information effectively and be able to communicate their ideas and thoughts effectively through their writing and speaking. As their teacher I am prepared to make the aspirations and dreams of students come alive through their writing as they try to entertain their peers.

CHAPTER 1

Skaters

Renee Clarke

There once was a sixteen year old girl named Kyria she had a dog named Spot and a cat named Whiskers. Kyria and Spot have so much in common; for one thing they love to roller skate and to skateboard. While on the other hand Whiskers does not have anything in common with either Spot or Kyria but she still loves to watch them play. Kyria's best friend Aiden was also sixteen she loves winning and skateboarding. While Kyria and Ai den are walking to Kyria's house a paper drops on th e floor. "Hey look at this there is a competition at the skate park it says, you and your pet will be able to skate around and do some tricks and that the person that wins will get a **HUGE SURPRISE!!!"**

"Let's join" said Kyria in an eager voice. "We have to work to our fullest potential" Kyria said to Spot. "Benji and I are going to win" Aiden said in a positive attitude.

At the park Spot and Kyria are working really hard and having new ideas and tricks every step of the way. On the other side of the skate park there was Aiden and her dog Benji, watching Kyria's and spots every move. "Hey guys" Aiden says in a crude way. "Benji and I are going to win for sure!!" Kyria replies "Ok Aiden we heard you the first time you don't have to be so obnoxious were all going to try our best." Aiden's response is "Me! Obnoxious please, I know I'm going to beat you." Kyria says "we all need to be good sportsmen to everyone." While Aiden replies "Ye ah ok" With an attitude. As Kyria and Spot left to go home, Aiden was up to mischief. "We have to win Benji In an eager voice to Benji. "Spot is our big competition so we have to get rid of him." When Kyria and Spot arrive at home they are very worried about Aiden. "Hey Spot aren't you wondering about Aiden she has been acting crazy all day." Kyria says as Spot replies by shaking his head. "They probably think I am weird or something for wanting something very bad," replied Aiden to Benji.

At that moment Benji and Aiden were still at the skate park prac ticing. On the other hand Aiden had to think of a plan to get rid of Spot. "I got it!" yelled Aiden to Benji "We'll first lightly sneak behind the rink and unscrew some of Spots wheels and put oil on both of their skateboards so they do not think that we were just aiming for Spot they will think we are aiming for both Spot and Kyria." Whispered Aiden. "They're going down!" As Kyria and Spot start to put their ideas together Aiden and Benji are trying to get some ideas. "The competition is coming up today is Thursday and we have until Saturday to get at least one idea," In a worried tone replies Aiden. As everyone is trying there hardest Kyria and Spot see their neighbor Bob and his daughter Angela who is eight years old. "Are you ready for the big competition?" said Bob "I heard it is going to be a hard decision on who is going to win with all this competition going on." "I'm going to win!!" yelled Aiden who is all the way across the room. "What's up with her?" asked Angela as she is wobbling on the skateboard. "Hi Angela I didn't see you down there, well she is just too competitive," replied Kyria. As Angela is changing the subject "I want to be just like you, like how you ride on the skateboard." "Well, all you have to do is practice and be a good sportsman to everyone."

The next morning Kyria is still worried about Aiden. "Something is wrong with her she has never acted like this before in all the competition before she never ever did this. while Kyria is talking to Spot. Sitting on her porch just bringing in the breeze Kyria is relaxed and nothing can stop her from doing her best. While on the other hand Aiden is still upset that they do not have anything. Kyria, Spot, Aiden, and Benji went their separate ways and started practicing. "The competition is tomorrow and we still don't have anything." Said Aiden in a worried tone "That's it plan COMPETITION is a go." "When Kyria and Spot go and buy some water we will do the plan, got it," said Aiden to Benji while Benji nods with an evil smirk on his face. Across from the skate park there is Bob and Angela. "You got it sweetie just keep trying," as Bob is encouraging his daughter. "I got it dad!!" While Angela is very anxious to learn her father starts video taping her roller skating, he sees something else, he sees Aiden purposely sabotaging Kyria and Spots skateboards. Bob and Angela go home and watch the tape to see if it was really Aiden and Benji because their video camera was a little blurry. As Kyria and Spot go back to their skateboard Aiden whispers "This is going to work," but Aiden can not whisper to good so Kyria replies "What did you say, what is going to work?" As Kyria and spot get ready to go down the ramp their skateboards start to shake. "What's going on why is this happening?" While Aiden and Benji have an evil smirk on their faces Kyria looks over and she knew that Aiden had something to do with it. Kyria and Spot fall to the ground and Spot starts to moan and weep. Kyria picks Spot up and just started looking at Aiden with a mean look. "I know you had something to do with it and you're going to get it."

At the vet the doctor t ells Kyria that Spot is ok he will just have to stay in a cast for a few days. "Ok doctor thank you." Walking home with whiskers Kyria starts to say "I'm going to need a replacement for Spot in the competition so get all the animals you know." Kyria changes the subject to Aiden as whiskers is already leaving. "I can't believe Aiden did this we use to be friends I know she did it now all I need is proof." Kyria is at home pacing to see if she can find the right animal to replace Spot who could learn all the tricks in one day. Kyria went through a whole lot of animals but she can't find one animal. Whiskers is just lying there as the animals keep coming in. Whiskers see that no one can replace Spot so whiskers sends all the animals home as Kyria calls "Next," Whiskers goes to Kyria and do all the tricks. "I know that you do not like the same thing as Spot and I but I know you want to help me, right." Kyria hugs whiskers tight as he is nodding his head yes. Kyria and Whiskers went to another skate park that Aiden does not know about so they can practice. "Now that Spot is out of the way we can practice and I would win, again." Aiden and Benji are at the skate park by themselves and they finally have some ideas and good tricks.

The day of the competition everyone is nervous except Kyria. "Were going to win were going to win!!" says Aiden in a confident voice. As everyone is waiting to see if Kyria is going to show or not Bob is still at home watching the video and looking at all the facts. "Who would want to win so badly they will injure another player?" said Bob "Who is very competitive?" He kept on asking himself these questions over and over until…. "Daddy the person that hurt Spot is Aiden," replied Angela. The players start to skateboard and there is no sign of Kyria. "She is not going to show just face it" said Aiden. The first contestant goes until it is Aiden's turn, which is when Spot comes, and then Kyria and then Whiskers. "I chose my cat, Whiskers to be my partner today because Spot is injured," Said Kyria. "Your cat!!" Aiden says in a shocking surprise. As Bob is driving to the skate park, he forgot about the video tape so he has to go back and get it. Bob says "This is a wonderful time to practice roller skating to the skate park ok Angela and try to stall." "Sure dad," said Angela.&nbs p; While Angela is almost at the park Aiden starts her first trick with Benji and everyone is surprised. Angela is at the park she ran to go tell Kyria the proof and that she needs a distraction. "I'll do it," replied Kyria. Aiden was almost finished with her turn until Angela and her small voice came out screaming "Does anyone want to know what happened to Spot, because I do." Kyria adds in "I heard someone unscrewed his wheels and the person put oil on both of our skateboard." "I'm trying to skate," said Aiden. Bob finally reaches the skate park "I have evidence of who injured Spot and the person will have to be disqualified from the competition, come and look," said Bob. They showed everyone the video and everyone was shocked to see that her own best friend betrayed her. "I did not want to be in this race anyway, I had plenty more things to do." Said Aiden "Then go do what you think is more important to you," replied Kyria. It was finally Kyria's turn to skateboard and she was doing tricks that know one has every seen before. Aiden did not actually leave she hid behind a bush so she can see what Kyria's tricks were. Out of all of this Angela learned how to roller skate and she20said "she was going to be in the next competition." Spot is all better Aiden is trying to keep her competitive streak down and Kyria won the huge surprise which was a brand new car. Everyone was happy with joy, but outside the skate park there was bitterness. Aiden learned her lesson to always treat people with respect.

CHAPTER 2

Treasure of the Dead

Ashley Bomar

"Get out of bed! We are going to be late for your aunt's funeral!" shouted Anna's mom. They are already 45 minutes late when they woke up. "We are already late." Anna said in a sleepy voice while crawling out of the bed. When Anna got out and checked the time, it was 10:45 a.m. Anna quickly jumped out of the bed and ran to the bathroom to brush her teeth and wash her face. When she was done, she ran into the room to change her clothes. It was 11:20 when Anna and her mom were ready to leave for the funeral. When they got to the funeral, Anna and her mom tried to get to the front of the crowd to see their beloved relative, dead in the coffin. "Excuse me! That is my sister in the coffin and I need to see her before she is buried!" shouted Anna's mom trying to get in front of the enormous crowd that was crowding around the coffin. Anna's mom was trying to get in front of the crowd, but Anna was just wondering around reading to names on the headstones. Then she noticed that one headstone said:

Put in a quarter
Go in and explore
And probably
You will get back,
A million,
more

This seems really interesting, thought Anna. She had a quarter and she thought that if she thought that if she goes in and explore then she will get a lot of money back. It sounds like I have to explore and find a very valuable treasure. Plus, I L-O-V-E exploring and adventures, thought Anna. After thinking about it, Ann slipped her hand into her purse and toke out a quarter, but before she could put the quarter into the slot, her best friend, Mary, jumps up behind her and questioned her, "what are you doing?" "I am about to put a quarter into the slot on this slot until you came." replied Anna.

Mary read the poem on the headstone and thought that the idea of going exploring would be cool, so she told Anna that it would be a great idea. After thinking about it again, Anna proceeded to put the quarter in to the slot. When she put the coin in, a big passage way that had stairs going in to it opened up. Anna stepped on to the stairs, and Mary followed her down. When Anna got down she looked around. She saw that there was a boat and something that looks like a piece of paper in a corner. She walked to the corner. "What are you doing?" asked Mary. "Wait by the boat, I am doing something," answered Anna.

Anna approached the object in a slow and cautious manner. Then she bent down to pick up the object, it was a treasure map being covered by sand. "Oh my gosh," said Anna," Come look at this Mary. I found the treasure map." Mary ran to Anna as fast a she possibly could. When she saw the map, she grabbed it away from Anna and walked toward the boat. "It says that we take the boat straight to Fruit Island." She said. "Ok then, let's go!" Anna said in a very excited voice. Then they both started to run toward the boat. Then they jumped on and started to row toward Fruit Island.

It was about 30 minutes when Anna and Mary got really hungry. They both started to look to see if there were any foods hidden around the small boat." Look what I found," shouted Mary, "a compass and an object that looks kind of like a telescope." Anna stepped up to Mary and asked if she could see the two objects. When Mary handed her the telescope like object, she looked threw it and saw that Fruit Island was a few meters away. "Look! I see the island!" Anna shouted on the top of her lungs. She was so happy that they were actually on a real treasure hunt.

When the boat hit the island, the two girls jumped out of the boat and ran to get the fruits; they grabbed and snatched everything they could. They even stopped on the island to eat a little before they start sailing again. When Anna and Mary were done packing the boat with the food, it was filled with fruits like strawberries, kiwis, lemons, bananas, cherries, and a whole lot more.

Then they stared sailing to the next island, which was called on the map, Monster Island. They were smooth sailing until Mary looked up and saw a shark fin circling the boat. Then she stared to see a lot more. Mary started to scream in horror and try to wake up Anna which was sleeping quietly on the side of the boat with her head hanging over so that the sharks could reach. Mary quickly got to Anna before the sharks did and pulled her over. Then she woke her up and showed her the sharks. Then one shark jumped over the boat and Anna took the rows and hit the sharks which made the sharks very angry. Then she took some fruits and cut herself and put some blood on the fruits then threw the fruits into the water. Then the sharks started to follow the fruits. Then Anna and Mary sailed by to the island.

When the boat got to the island, Anna and Mary sneaked out of the boat. Then they sneaked over to the brushes when they heard loud slow thumps coming toward them. When they saw the monster, they were scared out of their mind. Mary nearly fainted. Anna saw the key to the chest around the monsters neck on a chain." how are we supposed to get the key now?" Mary asked." Stay here I will get it. Then Anna ran out of the bushes, took up a very long piece of bamboo and stuck it in to a hole then used the bamboo stick to help her jump and stick her landing. She when she was in the air, she reached for the key around the monster's neck and landed on the ground. Then she screamed for Mary to run with her into the boat while the monster was chasing them from the island. Then they started to sail to the treasure chest which is on a small island that only it could fit on.

Then when Anna and Mary were almost there to the treasure chest, an enormous squid and a medium sized octopus leaped out of the water trying to destroy the boat. Then Anna took up a row and hit the octopus and the octopus sunk. Then Mary took the compass and threw it into the squid's eye and then the squid sunk.

When Anna and Mary got to the Treasure Island, they saw that the treasure chest had been guarded and the only way to get the treasure, they would have to name a lesson that they learned. "The lesson of… adventure?" Mary said. "The lesson of friendship." Anna said correcting Mary. Then she gave Mary a hug and called her, her b.f.f. which means best friends forever. And Mary said "B.F.F." then the treasure chest opened and Mary and Anna took the treasure and divided it in half and then the magically appeared in the graveyard where the funeral was still going on.

Then everyone noticed them and asked them where they got the treasure and they said absolutely nothing about the adventure they have been on.

CHAPTER 3

Zathura (The Unknown)

For Matt life was just average; Girls, football and regular high school dilemmas. Sadly he didn't know what was coming for him. Zathura (the Unknown)'s future was in his hands. Zathura was called the unknown planet because some didn't believe in its existence. It had just been hit by a huge meteor shower, which had left everyone divested, but alive because of King Cedric's heroic actions. Now it's up to Matt to succeed King Cedric, and rule Zathura and its people.

"Mom, where's my Abercrombie jeans? "Matt said as he ruffled through his dirty hamper. Matt's Mother Lisa walked over to his room from the couch where she had been watching her daily soap operas, Dangling his jeans in her right hand and replied with a little of sarcasm in her voice, "Only where you left them, of course ." Matt looked up then smirked, dropped the clothes in his hands onto his bed where the rest of piles of clothes he mounted on while looking for his jeans were. He walked over and grabbed his jeans and slipped them on quickly while saying "Right, red couch I believe?" Lisa gave a quick nod and tied her hair up. "So where are you two love birds going tonight?" Lisa questioned, referring to Aimee,

Matt's girlfriend of 2 years. Matt scratched his head while walking over to the kitchen and called back, "well I was thinking Fridays ...being that they always have some kind of special on Friday nights ." Lisa walked back to the kitchen and tossed a matching Abercrombie shirt to her son. Then replied "But it's up to Aimee huh?" Matt nodded while lacing his green and orange Ed Hardy's that Aimee bought for him 2 months ago. "Bye Mom, I love you" Lisa was know on the couch wrapped up in this week's episode of General Hospital. Just as the door slammed behind Matt, Lisa called back to him "I love you too, try and get home before 2" but after too it all become murmurs.

Back in Zathura everything and everyone was hectic. King Cedric's death due to saving Zathura and its people, left everyone in mourning. Queen Zenobie was now the ruler until the chosen one was revealed. Until then Zathura and those who live within the planet were due to misery. "Queen Zenobie my master what shall I get thee?" The Queen sat up from her thrown and walked over to her husband's loyal servant Charlie who worked for the king for over 15 years and felt the lose just as much as his wife. "I only need one thing" She said as she looked up with a somewhat evil look in her eye. "For you to fetch me the Chosen one". As she said these words the look in her eyes changed to a more pathetic helpless one and she walked away off into the darkness of the night .So Charlie did as he was told he ran back to the other servants and told them the news. It was up to them to find Sir Erwin, the only one within miles who knew how to Determine who the Chosen one was and where he or she was.

Meanwhile Back on Earth Matt was on his way to pick up Aimee When to his surprise he found a strange goldish quarter fall into his lap. Except this was no ordinary quarter. It was Bigger than a usual quarter and it was gold. He Waited for The Next Light to pick it up and when he did. He was so fascinated for he had never seen anything on it. He quickly slipped it into his pocket and drove away. As He appeared in Aimee's driveway, so did Karen, Aimee's Mother. "Hello Mrs. Wencher "Matt Greeted her with a quick hug." Hello to you to my darling." She replied as she pushed back her elegant, sleek black long hair. "Aimee's in her room getting ready" She said as she slipped right into her 2007 Benz. "Au Revoir" And off She was.

Matt Ruffled through his hair and walked up the driveway and into the 4 story house. "Well hello there" Aimee said as she strolled down the hallway to greet Matt. Matt looked up and smiled. He thought to himself, what a lucky guy am I. She ran up to him and he engulfed her into his arms and to follow up gave her a warm, soft, short but slow kiss.

"Can I take your order?" A tall and slim lady with hair up to her back had been taking their order or at least trying. Aimee put her menu down, flipped back her hair then said "Yes I would like a cheeseburgers with curly fries on the side and a sprite.." then looked over at Matt who was zoned out. "And for the gentlemen?" The lady, Annabelle to be précis had asked. Matt was still blanked out so Aimee gave him a little shove. "Oh um.. Yeah same as her except onion rings." Matt replied then went back to his quiet persona he had been putting on ever since he found the quarter in his car. Then Just as Matt was heading to the Bathroom, A relatively short man addressed him by the name Matt Rehar. "Um Excuse me?" Matt replied questioningly. The Short man moved closer and held on to his hand. Matt tried to hold back, but it was too late. Back in Zathura everyone was still miserable but everything got quiet as soon as Sir Erwin appeared with Matt Rehar, the Successor of King Cedric. Rehar was what a successor of a king was called in Zathura. "Welcome to your kingdom" replied Erwin. Matt looked confused and started yelling and stuff. Erwin was gone again and then reappeared with everyone he loved back on Earth in Zathura. Everyone was confused, but at dinner everything was explained to them. They had no choose, they were being imprisoned if they didn't cooperate. So they agreed and after awhile everything was just about as normal. Matt and Aimee got married and became King and Queen of Zathura. Zathura and its people couldn't be any happier with any other king and queen.

THE END !!!!

CHAPTER 4

A World with Giants

Fleurika Ambroise
July 13, 2009

This story is about a little girl who wanted soda but was banned because the giant banded it. What will happen to the girl? Will she ever g et back her soda? The only way to find out is to read the rest of the story. It starts in a world with people and then that's when the giants come in they own all the world accept for new York and they planned on getting it and capturing all the people in it.

The giant are trying to take over the world they already took over half the universe and are coming closer and closer to America they have captured kids from other countries and are planning on capturing more there kids they can't fight but not Annie she is a tough girl that will fight for anything you cross the line when you play with her soda no matter what it takes she will get here soda that is Annie.

Now the giants have invaded New York accept for the part that the little girl lived in witch was Manhattan were a little girl went to the corner store looking for soda when she had entered the shop and asked the man said there was no soda she screamed and screamed and begged to see the manager and the said he had it but could not sell it or he would be killed by the giants. So she said ok and left the shop. Knowing, that one day she will get her soda and if it had to be a fight so she could get the soda she would get it. She walks out and a man try to kidnap her while she is walking to the train station. She runs into the train before it can go making sure that the guy does not get in. While she is in there she finds a bottle of soda in the bottom of the chair in the train and when she is not looking a man try's to take it from her she opens it and throws it at him so he does not get her and take the soda away. She jumps of the train right on her stop and runs home the guy was still in the train so he could not follow her. While she runs decides to stop buy the park and walks around the park. It is right near her house so she does not have to worry about anything coming after her. She wonders where she got that soda.

Annie said to herself I have to think of a way to stop those boneheads who took away my soda and stop them from taking over the world wait a minute the soda that's it when I threw the soda at the man he shrieked he must have been a giant ok I have to think of something and I have to think fast OK what do I do? let's think I will make an army of clones and build them with soda and shrink the giants once and for all the only problem is where am I going to get clones or even worse soda oh I got it when I was on the train I pulled soda from out of the under of the train seats will get them from the train seats now there is only on e thing left where do I get the clones? OK think I'll go to the factory and asked them to build clones out of soda that's it. So she went and asked the factory to do it and they did it gladly.

She fought a courageous fight she fought it was hard and she had trouble but in the end she won all those evil giants died in the woods of darkness in the end the girl was rewarded with a large three truck supply of soda and she saved the little kids and all the people in the whole entire world and the giants promised they would never ever be mean to little kids ever again and the soda was restored to the people of America and the rest of the world and the story of how she saved the world and tough the giants a lesson and restored the soda and no one would ever take the precious soda away from the world of ANNIE.

CHAPTER 5

The Ward of Agony

Jack Yung

The ward just gives me the shivers down my spine, even the trees rustling, and the hollowing wind in a crisp autumn; I still tremble when looking at this monstrous building that soars up to seven floors. I don't really enjoy visiting here, but my friend Boris does community service here. I am Thomas Wilkes, an eighteen year old still in college. I can't believe my friend works here. The disabled people act very strange when you are near them. After I chatted with Boris, I quickly left to hang out with my other friends Catherine, Gilliam, and Tracey.

The sky was darkened and I just realized that I left my backpack in the reception desk. My essay is due tomorrow, so I had to get it. So, I asked all my friends to come with me to retrieve it. Boris was found near the opposite sidewalk and I asked him to come with me too. He rejected my offer and rushed home, some friend he is. My head started to ache when I approached the ward again. I busted the creaking door and went inside. The floors creaked every time and the darkness shrouded us like a foggy mist. As I grabbed my backpack the door slammed with full force and someone locked us inside. This got to be a trick or is it?

We tried banging with all our might but, it won't even budge. The group decided to split up, Catherine went with me and Gilliam went with Tracey. We had to find an exit and fast because this place creeps me out. Catherine was a pain in the neck and kept complaining about how this place is so untidy. There were so many doors to check out, until finally there was a wooden door at the end of the hall which was locked. I didn't want to destroy property, but Catherine didn't bother so she smashed the door with a chair and unlocked the doorknob. This room was completely dark and musty. This was probably where the doctors meet at during their break. There was the stove and even a oven, probably a kitchen. Catherine moved her hand to the faucet and turned on the water to wash her hands. I found the light switch and turned it on to help illuminate the room. All of the sudden, Catherine screamed like a siren so I checked what was wrong. I was speechless and almost vomiting at what I saw.

Fresh blood dripped like a fountain as I reached and opened the shelf for a towel. Human flesh and bones dangled down rotting like a dead carcass as flies gathered around. The sight of the brain in the container made me cringe in fear because it looked like vanilla pudding that spilled out. Suddenly, a shadowy figure showed up in the hall as the lights died out. I hid around the corner of the table, trembling as he came closer to the room. I kept my mouth tight and sealed hoping I won't be his victim. Catherine cried out in fear and soon it died out in a moan…..

I quickly ran for my life and I rolled down the stairs without looking. "Ow, the pain in my head hurts and is throbbing like crazy." I needed to hide so no choice but, to choose any door with the first glance. I just decided to open the closet…hoping the killer doesn't find me here. In disgust, I saw Gilliam and Tracey hanging by a rope in the room. They were sliced by a scalpel, probably which made their intestines spill out like meat hanging in a factory. Now I was sure that I was alone in the dark. In the halls I roamed, and again then noticed a person in a wheel chair. Relieved, finally hope is here at last. "Hello there, please help me!" I cried.

The old man's face turned purple slowly and I walked a few steps back. Worms squirmed out of his ear and mouth. I slowly moved away even more and stepped on someone's shoe.

Turning around I saw a doctor and he shook his head. "It seems like you didn't have your operation yet kid…" he mumbled as he grabbed me by the shoulder. Everything went blank, empty, and cold. A sharp pain in my shoulder felt like a stab from a knife. A few minutes later I saw lights flashing and a TV on as people were talking and moving around.

"Wake up are you okay, you almost gave me a heart attack. You shouldn't go outside by yourself now, this is your home so don't go anywhere without my permission." It was Boris, as he gave me my pills; he sighed and started to tell me about the incident I had when I was little. I had a defect when I was little that made me get nightmares every time I sleep, that is why I need my pills. So the truth is this nightmare never happened because I think I forgot to take my pills today, My bad…..

CHAPTER 6

Spiders

Juliana Sempertegui

Intro: One sunny day Karla, Carly's little sister, Freddy, Carly's boyfriend, Carly and their friends, Margarita, Jeremy, Alice, Jonathan and Ashley were flying back to new Ashley were flying back to New York from Japan. When they were on the plane, they were excited by all the souvenirs they purchased in Japan. They couldn't wait to get back to New York; they were all hyper. It was night already and they were still flying through Asia. They all fell asleep and had sweet dreams. When the plane landed somewhere in Europe they hopped off and transferred themselves to the plane that was headed to New York. When they got to the plane they were wondering why nobody else was on the plane, but they didn't know that spiders were waiting for them in New York…

P#1: When the plane landed all Margarita, Jonathan, Jeremy, Freddy, Alice, Ashley, Carly, and Karla heard was screaming and yelling. "I wonder what's happening?" questioned Carly, "I don't know, but it sounds scary." responded Freddy. When they got off the plane all they saw was people running around like crazy and screaming. Then they suddenly saw huge, hairy legs. Carly gasped then fell backwards; luckily Freddy was in back of her and caught her. She was unconscious for half an hour. When Carly was back in conscious she asked "What happened?" "You fainted after seeing the humongous hairy legs the spiders." said a panicked Karla. "So what I saw was real? Where are the others?" asked Carly trying to sound relaxed." "They are up in Heaven living in peace" commented Freddy with a shiver. Carly started to cry thinking about her parents.

P#2: Freddy, Carly and Karla had to escape the cave they were hiding in, because apparently the big spiders laid eggs on the cave and the eggs were starring to open. They were trying to figure out a way to get out and get to a place where they would be saved with the coverage of food. "So where are we going to go again to be saved, without any of the weird creatures making us their dinner?" said Carly sarcastically. "Even when it's a terrifying moment you have to use that sarcasm…"started Karla, but she didn't get to finish because apparently a spider spotted them and the first one it grabbed was Karla. "No!!" screamed Carly, "We have to go before he gets one of us as well." said a terrified Freddy. All Carly did was nod her head because she was bursting into tears, she didn't know if she lost her parents, but in the end she knew she lost her sister.

P#3: At last Carly and Freddy ended up in a hotel. This hotel provided food, but no service. "We can't just stay here and do nothing for the rest of our lives." exclaimed Carly to Freddy. "I know that but what else can we do?" challenged back Freddy, "You know my uncle is scientist he can probably make a bomb that will kill all of the nasty beasts." suggested Freddy. "That's an impressive idea, but where can we find your uncle?" asked Carly with a worried expression, "He lives in France and he's a number one scientist; he can probably get here in a private yet." answered Freddy. "But how will we contact him then?" retorted Carly. Freddy didn't answer to that but he came up with something else. "I know! My dad was a bomb maker; we can probably make something out of that, because he thought some stuff." said Freddy excitedly.

They were going to have to go to Freddy's house, which probably like 5 blocks away from the hotel they were in. They went hiding every time they saw a spider close by; until they got there. "We are here…finally." said Carly sarcastically and with fear at the same time. "Stop joking Carly, now we have to go to my dad's lavatory. Follow me." whispered Freddy to Carly. They went down the basement escalators, and then they went down another set of stairs to get to the lavatory. When they got there they found Mr. Sanchez in the lavatory. "Dad your alive, I'm so glad!" exclaimed Freddy. "Yes I am, but your sister and mother aren't." said Mr. Sanchez with a sad expression. Freddy's tears started to burst out but he spoke normally anyway. "I'm sorry responded Carly. They remained in silence for a moment.

P#4: "Dad can you make a bomb to destroy the spiders once in for all?" questioned Freddy with an immense anger. "I can build one but it will take at least 2 days and I would need a helper. We will also need a place to explode the bomb but with all the spiders in there." answered Mr. Sanchez. Carly came up with a significant idea, "What if we put some of the dead people that are already wrapped in the silk of the spider, and we put them in the cave me and Freddy were hiding in. Then we get the spiders attention and make them chase us into the cave. But to that we will need an escape line to escape run so the spider won't get us and make us their dessert." suggested Carly. Mr. Sanchez and Freddy both nodded with a grin on their face.

P#5: Two days passed and they all had it planned out already. Mr. Sanchez was putting the finishing touches to the cave and Freddy and Carly were planning everything else. "Okay, so Mr. Sanchez you have the biggest spiders which are three of them you won't have any trouble because they are the ones that stick together mostly. I and Freddy will get the rest of them; we won't have any trouble with the little ones because they are all inside the cave already. So all we have to do is bring them to the cave we get out through the little passages we made then we close all the doors and explode the bomb." planned Carly out loud. "Great idea

Carl's." pointed Freddy out. "Thanks." responded Carly blushing. It was starring to get dark, so before they went on to their mission they had to eat to get energy. The clock hit 7 pm; all the spiders were starting to come out, so Mr. Sanchez, Carly and Freddy were starting to get ready. "I think we're going to have fun." said Freddy excitedly; "Well I feel the same thing, but also a little scared." replied Carly.

P#6: "Okay run to run to cave as fast as you can, your dad is already there and the spiders are trying to get out!!!!" screamed Carly while running with Freddy over to the cave. The planned had worked so far and they gathered up as many spiders they can find. Suddenly they heard someone calling them, and they noticed it was Jeremy, Ashley and Alice. All Carly can think at the moment was 'yes there save' and then she concentrated back on getting to the cave. When Freddy and Carly got there they got in fast and got out fast. Luckily no spiders escaped the trapped and Mr. Sanchez closed every escape there was for them. Then Mr. Sanchez pushed the button and all the spiders died.

Conclusion: In the end every single meat-eater spider was dead. Everything got back to normal; Carly found her parents and told them about her sister, they did a funeral for Freddy's mom and for Karla. Jeremy, Alice and Ashley were happy they found their parents, and they found jobs to work in while the guy builders were fixing all damage that occurred. After two years they were all living together as one family even though they weren't and they lived pleased, for a while.

CHAPTER 7

Why I'm in Jail

Kyle R. James

A story of twins, a gun and Yankees tickets.

"You may see him now" the corrections officers said. "Oh my baby" Ron's mother said. "I told you he was going to jail, I told you" his father said. "Don't drop the soap," Cassie his sister said, "tie it to your hand, you do not want a prostate at 15." "What's a prostate?" I said. "It is when a man violates your butt," my father said. As you can tell I am in jail. Why? That's simple. I shot my girlfriend or ex-girlfriend. I know what you are thinking that I am evil to kill my girlfriend but it was by accident. I bet you would want to know what happened. Well! I am not telling you mind your business. "Ron, who are you talking to, my mom said". "I talking to them" I said. Oh! I did not see you there my eyes are filled with tears" she said, "why you don't tell them why you are in jail so they will not make the same mistake". "k!"

It all started at school, I had a girlfriend her name was Jasmine. We were in math class when she asked me to go to the movies with her. I said yes. I thought that we can go to the movies then go to her house for some FUN. I walked home from school alone. Jasmine did not walk home with me. She said she is busy. "Yo! Ron I got the tickets" Said Dev. "What tickets" I said. The tickets for the last Yankees game at Yankee stadium". "Your "gassing" it, shows me" I said. There they were at the last game, but it was on the same day as my date with Jasmine.

I pulled out his 'kick' and called Jasmine. I lied; I told her that he had to go to the 'doc'. She believed me, and Dev and I went to the game. I brought my Yankees hat, Yankees shirt, Yankees jean, and Yankees shoes. At the game, Dev and I sat next to each other. When "A-rod" was up to bat, I felt that he was going to hit a "home run". Suddenly, I heard the crowd screaming then everybody started jumping that when they got up. I saw the ball coming towards me. I jumped to catch the ball, but it went behind me. Some guy caught it, and gave it to a girl. I heard him say this is for you for our ninth month anniversary, JASMINE. I turned around and it was my Jasmine.

The next day at school, I asked Jasmine for a date, she said yes. I took her to see a movie, and then to the park. It was dark, and the only thing we saw were the moon light. We held hand; I asked her if she would you ever cheat on me she said no. That is when he told her that I saw her at the Yankee's game with another male. She denied it. I was very angry all the love I had for her turned into pain. I took out my gun with the intention to make her afraid suddenly the gun misfired and shot her.

I started to cry. While Jasmine lay on the ground dying, I heard a voice said Jasmine! I looked around, and saw the guy that was at the Yankee's game with a girl that looked identical to my Jasmine. I felt like a fool. I killed an innocent person. Minutes later, the cops arrested me. I received life in prison. Why Jasmine's parents did give identical twins the same name?

The End

CHAPTER 8

Brendon's Restoration

By: Alejandro Ruiz

Chapter 1:
Utter Destruction: Demise

Good morning Alex." said Billy. "Oh good morning Billy." replied Alex."I think I'll just go outside today." When Alex got outside, his friends Zack and Drake told him about Brendon. "Alex did you hear about Brendon?" asked Zack. "He went to challenge that chaos being!" added Drake."What?! We have to go and help him!" said Alex.

When everyone arrived at the tower, Zack asked "Wow when did this tower fall?" "You mean you don't know?" started Alex. "When that chaos being was still human I challenged him." "Then he was going to cast a spell on me but I had a magic mirror that reflected it. After that he tried to turn me into a frog and he turned himself into one. So I guess the being is his spirit." "Does that mean you can beat his spirit?" asked Drake.

"Probably, luckily, he doesn't have his staff anymore." replied Alex.

The party went through the portal and got to the chaos being. Although, when they got there, the chaos being disappeared and Brendon was found dead. "Oh no were too late!" started everybody." Now what?" asked Zack. "We're not going to let it end like this!" said Alex. "We'll have to go to Death's realm."

Chapter 2:
Through the Portal and On to life: A Dragon's Guidance!

"Did something hit you on the head on the way here?" asked Drake. "I'm serious, and I've been there twice." Although Death is pretty angry since I tried to bring someone back to life before and I tried to take his guard dog's baby." said Alex. "Okay... well at least we know we can get there." said Zack. "We should probably go to the ancient ruins since it goes directly to Death." said Alex.

When the party got to town, they found a portal. "How convenient, a portal in the middle of town that goes to the ruins." said Zack. "Oh, I opened that so that we can get to the ruins faster. Too bad I can't open one to Death's realm. The guard dog will kill us in a sec if we go through that portal." explained Alex. "Whatever let's just go." said Drake.

"It's a good thing I killed all those machines that were here last time." said Alex. "Hey the portal is over there!" exclaimed Zack. "Wait, be cautious." said Alex. Then a blue spirit came out of the portal. "Who are you?" asked Drake. "I guess you could say I'm an evil dead guy." said the blue spirit. "Whoever you are, let us go through the portal!" said Zack. "You'll have to beat me first." said the spirit.

Drake starts by throwing a knife at the spirit, but it gets reflected! Drake's parrot attacks it but only light can hurt it! Drake dodges the knife and uses a light bomb. The spirit uses a blue fire against the light bomb. The fire is so strong that it's enough to destroy the light bomb and hit Drake! The blast was to powerful for Drake to survive...

"No!" cried Alex and Zack. The spirit shoots another fireball but Zack fades and Aero, Alex's dragon deflects it with a beam of light. The spirit gets hurt a bit and Zack uses his Ninja Death Strike. The spirit engulfs himself in flames and Zack gets hurt by the flames. The spirit finishes him with a pulse of darkness.

"That's it!" yelled Alex, "Now you're finished!" Alex uses a shied to weaken the spirit's attacks. Then he summons a fire dragon spirit! The spirit uses his blue fire but it just makes the dragon spirit stronger. "Now to finish this, Dragon Heart!" yelled Alex. Wings grew and Alex starts to fly. He strikes with a blue energy which defeats the spirit but destroys the ruins as well! Luckily Alex goes through the portal just in time.

Chapter 3:
Risen Again to Fight the Undead: The Return of Brendon

Alex enters the portal and quickly finds his friends. "Oh good I found you guys fast." started Alex. "You won't be able to do anything here so leave it to me. Then suddenly Death appears. "You know what let's just get this over with so don't start yelling." said Alex.

Alex summons an earth dragon spirit, which creates an earthquake. Death uses a dark pulse with his scythe like the other spirit. Then Death heads straight for Alex so he doesn't have a choice. He has to use his necromancer powers to bring his friends back. "Time to kick some dead butt!" said everybody.

Drake uses his knife again but Death uses his scythe to stop it. Zack uses his sword, moves very quickly and attacks Death with a powerful blast. Finally Brendon uses his Phoenix and it creates a powerful blast that defeats Death. "Wow we-" starts Zack but gets interrupted. "Why don't we leave first, oh and thanks." said Brendon.

Chapter 4:
Stealth of a Paladin: Revenge All Over!

The party gets in and Brendon is last, but just then Death pops up again! "No I won't let you escape!" exclaimed Death. He shoots a beam that closes the portal. Then he just disappears. "Oh great now I have to find another way out." thought Brendon. Just then whole bunches of undead come to fight Brendon. "Oh how annoying these undead can be." thought Brendon. "I know I'll just blind them all." Brendon illuminates the whole place and the undead get hurt a bit, plus the light is too strong for them to see. Brendon quickly sneaks past them and finds the other portal out.

He then realizes that the portal lead to the chaos being's tower! "How convenient, I get a rematch." "Oh good you made it out. Well if you're going to fight then hurry." said Alex.

Alex, Aero, Zack, Drake, Brendon and his phoenix use their most powerful attacks and they defeat the chaos being. "Well that was boring." said Brendon. "So you wanted to die? Besides I said make it quick." said Alex "Fine lets go home" said Brendon. Just then the chaos being's son came in. "What, what did you do to my father, again!" "Oh well this is not good" said Alex. "That's one ugly son." said Zack. "The chaos being has a son?" asked Drake. "Now you die!" said the son. He uses an explosion of darkness while Alex uses his blue energy explosion. "The tower is starting to collapse; we have to get out of here!" said Brendon. They went through the portal but so did the son. "I'll get you if it's the last thing I do…" said the son as the tower got destroyed.

CHAPTER 9

JUMPER 2

There once was a father named Chuck Jones. He and his 7-year-old son James Jones just moved into a new home, after Anna Jones left him. He didn't want to live in a house where there were memories of his beloved wife; to him it was too painful. When Anna left she said that someday she would come back to take James with her. She never did. Instead she died of cancer. In her will she asked her sister Heather to look after him. Chuck on the other hand thought that James would be happier with him instead. After a week of discussion they came to a decision that James would choose who to live with. James never came to a decision, so James stayed with his dad until he could.

It was 9:00pm and James' bedtime. "Hey Dad will you read me this book I picked up from the school library." asked James. "Sorry son, I would love to but I have to go over some papers for the office tomorrow. How about tomorrow night?" replied Chuck. "Fine, but this time do you pinky swear that you will read it to me?" asked James. "Well I can't pinky swear that I will but I can pinky swear that I will try." replied Chuck. Chuck said goodnight to James and went to his room to do his work.

The next day when James came back from school he said, 'Uh….. Dad, what would you do to me if I had a bad grade science, but said I would do better in school?" "James every time you say that it means you didn't even try……Ok let's see what you won on the punishment wheel! Drum roll please……Congratulations you won one week of garbage duty!" said Chuck in a sarcastic voice. "OK Dad you can keep laughing now but I got an A+ in Math!" cheered James. "That's great! This means I can read that Martian story to you. What was the name of it again?" "Galactico vs. Quarzon." said James.

When James went to go get the book he remembered that his dad had to go to work late that night. "Dad don't you have to go do surgery tonight?" asked James.

"Oh man I completely forgot about that. Um …. I'll have to read it to you later I'll try to get home before 10:00 alright. I'll call Amber to come look after you" said Chuck. Amber was James' babysitter who used to make him do all sorts of chores like washing the dishes and cleaning his room. It wasn't that hard but he couldn't stand her. But that all change after she was married to a psychologist named Adam. Chuck looked at his watch and noticed that he was going to lat e for work.

"Calling Dr. Jones, Calling DR. Jones." said the secretary on the loudspeaker. Chuck got his uniform and performed a heart transplant. "Scalpel….Knife…. swab…"Ordered Chuck. The surgery went on for at least two hours, when he was done he explained to the patient what medicine that he should take. On his way out from the hospital Chuck was walking down the street and found a gypsy selling apples; he was very hungry and wanted that apple badly. "Hey I would like one apple please" said Chuck. "These apples are for free but heed my words if you choose to eat the apple mystical powers shall come upon you." replied the gypsy in an eerie voice. "Hey lady, Halloween is not till next month, I just want my dam apple". "Yes you may have the fruit but you were warned" whispered the gypsy. Just then, Chuck ran to the car knowing that it was very late and that he may have to pay Amber overtime. When he arrived home he went into the house quietly knowing that James was sleeping. "James and I had a wonderful time Mr. Jones; I made him dinner, played games, watched a movie and made sure that he was in bed by ten o'clock." explained Amber. "Great, how much do I owe you for tonight?" asked Chuck. "Well, it is ten dollars per hour so you owe me ninety dollars; and by the way James was telling me that you were supposed to read him a story, he seemed very disappointed so I asked him if I could read the story to him. He said that he wanted to spend time with you." replied Amber. "Well things come up, I can`t promise him everything." said Chuck in a firm voice. "Ok but don`t tell that to me, try telling it to James and now I have to go, Adam is waiting for me at home." said Amber. As Amber walked out through the door, Chuck was looking through some papers found in his bag. Chuck was looking around the kitchen knowing that there was no dinner left for him. Chuck went through his pocket and found the apple he had from the strange gypsy. Chuck pulled it out of his pocket and took a big bite out of it. "I don`t know what this lady was talking about; this is a good apple" said Chuck talking to himself. When he went to bed; he had a little tickle in his stomach and little did he know what he was about to expect in the morning.

"Oh, my stomach, I should never have had that apple late at night." Chuck got out of his bed and tripped over a medical book on the floor. When he got off the floor, he found out that he was not in his room at all." Oh my God, where the heck am I?!" Chuck was shock to see a world of surgical equipment around him. He was running around the book looking for a way out. While he was so busy looking for a way out, he noticed three floating scalpels coming toward him. He jumped three times and out of the book on the floor of his bedroom. When Chuck got up he went straight to James room tell him about his experience.

"James. Get up, right now!!!" yelled Chuck. "What happen? Is there a fire?" asked James "This may seems a little strange, but this morning I literally felt into one of my medical book; if you do not believe, well jump into your story book." said Chuck all excited.

He grabbed James' arm and jumped into James' story book. "Wow at first I thought you were crazy but this is so cool!!!!" Said James. He saw piles of red rocks and little green Martians just like the ones he saw in the pictures. "You want to know what's really crazy. I think this happened last night when I took that apple from a creepy gypsy. She said it had magical powers and now I have them." Explained Chuck. "Well if were in the book wouldn't that mean Galactico is here? If so that also means that Quarzon is here to. So we have to be careful." warned James. While Chuck and James were discussing ways to stay safe and where to find Galactico; Quarzon was making up his own plan.

"For the sake of my planet, who are these strangers and why have they come? Anox explain to me who these things are." Ordered Quarzon. "Well by the data in the navigator it seems that these creatures came out of know where. The tall one claims to be showing that little one our planet, but they don't seem to be much of a threat to us." Explained Anox. "Well then, if he wants a tour will give one. Guards I want you to capture them and bring them back to my tower! Now!" yelled Quarzon.

"Hey did you here something?" asked Chuck. Chuck and James heard some sort of growl behind a mountain. They turned around thinking it was safe but they were wrong. All of a sudden all of Quarzon's minions jumped out and attack them. James was too weak to fight (considering that he didn't eat breakfast) and was an easy target. Chuck did the best to fight them off. He punched and kicked but it was too late. James was captured. Chuck was then knocked out and was tied to a boulder.

When Chuck woke up he looked around to find his son. But there was no luck. While Chuck was worrying about his son a large shadow appeared over his shoulder. "Who are you and what do you want?" asked Chuck in a scared voice. "What do you mean? You don't know who I am?" said the stranger in a heroic voice. Chuck turned around a saw a large man with muscles in a red, blue and green costume. "I am Galactico, protector of Mars." Said the hero. "Really? If your Galactico, would that mean you can help me defeat Quarzon and help me rescue my son?" asked Chuck. "Of course! And I did hear about that. It must be really hard to go through this but never fear we are going to rescue him." Said Galactico.

Back at the tower James was locked up in a cell crying. "I hope dad will come back. I want to go home." Said James in a sad voice. While James was doing his sobbing Quarzon came in and said…. "Hmmm…..I only see one of them. Where is the other one?" said

Quarzon. "The other one is still out there we have failed you master." Said the Guard. "This is true, but your stupidity made me an idea. The tall one will eventually want to reclaim this one. When he does he will fall into his despair." Said Quarzon "But master these creatures look like they mean harm destroying them would be pointless." said Anox. "Who said I was going to destroy them. There is no way these things would come here on their own. They must have some sort of power that allowed them to come. If I drain that power will be invincible." Explained Quarzon James couldn't believe what he just heard. He had to find some way to warn his dad. He had a piece of paper in his pocket and a pencil on the floor. James took his hand and tried to make a message, but it was no use. His hands were chained to the wall. So James came up with an idea and used his toes to make words. It wasn't his best work, but it was good enough. He saw a window across from him and used his foot to throw it out the window. It made it, so all James could do was hope that his dad would get the message.

Chuck and Galactico ventured on toward Quarzon's castle. They faced horrible monsters and aliens, avoided asteroids, and managed to dodge cosmic explosions. Chuck got stronger but Galactico turned weaker until he was unable to fight any longer. "Chuck go on without me I will be fine but James won't if you don't save him. The castle is straight ahead." Said Galactico. "Thank you and don't worry I will come back." replied Chuck. As Chuck slipped past the guards at the gate he crept into the room where they were keeping James. "Dad is that you? We have to get out of here there planning on draining your powers so we don't escape and so Quarzon can become very powerful." warned James. "Well don't worry I've got a plan." said Chuck. "You do?" asked James. "Yes! My plan is to run, find the hole to get back home and jump three times." Explained Chuck in a confident voice. "Nice plan. I think you can be a superhero one day. And I have a perfect name, Jumper."

They managed to escape without being detected. They found the hole and were about to jump until Quarzon found them! He sent his guards after them. They blasted laser beams and grabbed at James. Chuck kicked a blaster out of one of the guard's hand and began shooting. Chuck had excellent aim and was driving them off. "He is to strong retreat!!" yelled one of the guards. The guards left, but Quarzon jump out from a rock and battled with Chuck. Chuck blasted Quarzon in the head, grabbed James and jumped three times out of the book. "Someday I will have my revenge." said Quarzon.

James and Chuck look around the house making sure that they weren't followed. "So James what did you think of that?" asked Chuck. "I think that was way better then reading the book! And also tell Aunt Heather that I want to stay here with you." replied James. "Don't worry I will. Now let's go out for some pizza!" said Chuck. "Awesome! I'm starving." said James. Chuck and James spent the rest of the after noon traveling through more books. Through that day on James always referred to his dad as Jumper.

CHAPTER 10

Marshall The Martian

Warren Clarke

How would you like to learn about what life was like on Mars? For a Martian named Marshall, life would turn out to be way harder than he expected it to be. Marshall was not a very popular guy in Martianville; he didn't have many family members or many friends, and although he owned the Martianville Deli he rarely made much money because he didn't have many customers. It wasn't going to get any better for our friend Marshall.

The day began like any other normal day for Marshall. He woke up at 7:45 and got to the Martianville deli at around 8:15. Marshall was the only person who worked at the deli because all of his employees quit on him after about 3 days of work. Marshall didn't bother to hire anyone else after the fifth person quit. Marshall's first customer of the day was Madison; she was Marshall's neighbor, and his only friend. (Who Marshall secretly had a HUGE crush on)

"What'll it be today Madison"

"I'll take a medium cup of coffee please"

"Coming right up"

As Madison left with her coffee Marshall went to the room in the back of the store to get more cups. On his way back upstairs Marshall heard a loud crash. "Who's there?!" Marshall repeatedly asked, but when he heard no answer he had decided to go upstairs and figure out what the noise was. Even though he was scared to death of what could be upstairs, Marshall quickly dialed 911 on his cell phone and ran to the front of the store. When he saw that the glass windows and door were shattered and the money was stolen from the cash register. In shock Marshall dropped the phone; completely forgetting about calling the police as he began to carefully examining the Deli to make sure that nothing else was stolen. Then he thought "who would do such a thing?" he thought about it for a good 10 minutes and came up with three solutions, it was either one of the many employees he fired, over the past week (they hated his guts), Madison (which he highly doubted) or the most likely of all … Bob, he and Marshall went to high school together and they used to be the best of friends, but when Marshall turned his back on Bob and didn't help him take over the world, Bob never forgave him. Now they both hate each other and rarely ever talked to each other.

Marshall convinced himself that it was Bob who robbed his store. He decided not to call the police because he wanted to settle this dispute fair and square.

The next day Marshall went to Bob's house and pounded on the door. When Bob opened the door Marshall shouted "I know you were the one who robbed my Deli, and I'm going to get my revenge!" Bob just stood there with the most intimidating grin on his face and said, "I highly doubt that you'll be able to anyway, you're just not as cunning and smart as I am"

Marshall then left to think of an evil plan to get Bob back for robbing the deli. After about an hour Marshall came up with a brilliant idea of how he should get back bob for robbing his store.

Knowing that Bob also had a big crush on Madison Marshall went to her house to explain to her what he did, hoping that it would ruin his chances with her. When Marshall rang the door bell he kept going over what he would say so he didn't make a fool of himself in front of a girl he liked. Moments later Madison opened the door. "Good morning Marshall shouldn't you be at the deli right now?"

"That's the problem." Marshall said, "The Deli was robbed yesterday at around 9:00 and I have a strong suspicion that Bob was the one who did it" suddenly a look of guilt grew on Madison's face, as she stared at her feet she said, "Marshall, I was the one who robbed the Deli. I'm really sorry, but I really needed the money, please forgive me." Marshall stood there in shock; he was unable to believe that the love of his life would do such a thing to him. "H-H-how could you?" Marshall said, shaking.

Madison then closed the door without saying another word.

Marshall figured that he'd take the log way home, to clear his head. He was about a block away from home when he realized that the only Martian he loved only used him to get closer to money, and his best friend since high school hated him.

Marshall decided that his time was up in Martianville, and that he should move somewhere else and start again, make new friends, and possibly start a family. And that's exactly what he did.

CHAPTER 11

Revenge

Gaelin Linares
8th Grade

I stood on the corner of my block waiting for that rusty old streetlight to change. It's been broken for a while now, what kind of streetlight gets stuck on yellow for two minutes? Honestly, the second most hated thing in my life has to be that stupid streetlight. I crossed the street once the light had finally changed, the walk to Irra's house was short, but unfortunately I would still have to walk pass Mr. Jones… Oh joy. He has always hated me for some reason. It sucks that every time I have to pass his house, usually to go to Irra's, he is watering his lawn or cleaning his pool, or doing some other chore that normal people hate to do. The last time I passed his house he threw a newspaper at me, and it hit me square in the head. Old people are not supposed to have good aim. It's freaky.

As I approached his house, I sped up my pretty slow pace; I didn't want to be attacked by a newspaper… Again. I was directly in front of his house and I thought that maybe this time he was inside. Then I heard the flow of running water… Hooray. I assumed he was watering his lawn but I didn't stop to turn and look.

"You little…." I heard the grumpy voice of that short, balding old man that I have come to know and hate. "I told you never to come by my house again!"

I turned my head, just slightly, to, make sure he didn't have a newspaper in his hand, or anything heavier for that matter. Just my luck he had something in his hand, it was unidentifiable from this distance. All I could decipher about the object was that it looked fairly round.

He raised his arm and threw the object at me. It landed directly near me at my feet. I just stared at it for a few seconds then I bent over to pick it up. It was jet-black rock with some strange markings on it. It must have been one of those artificial souvenir rocks that you see in those tourist shops. I tossed it up and caught it in my other hand and chuckled. Well that's the aim that a sixty-year-old man is supposed to have.

"Nice aim old man!" I yelled to him as I continued to approach Irra's house. I wondered if Seth and Lana were there to… Once I finally got to the gate to her house, I opened it and approached the front door. Just as I raised my fist to knock on the door, it swung open, and I ended up knocking on Seth's head instead.

Oops.

He just blinked at me twice as I snickered at him. That had to be the highlight of my entire life so far.

"So now you know how hollow my head is." He said, smiling and walking past me and toward Irra's lawn set. Irra appeared at the doorstep with a monster-sized bag of chips and three super sized cups of coke. They looked extra bubbly so she probably shook them before she opened them, as usual. Looking at that bag of chips made me hungry. I stuck my hand out toward the bag and right as I was about to grab it Irra slapped my hand away.

"What was that for?!" I asked. A little confused actually.

"I get the first chip," she explained happily.

"You devious little gremlin" I said laughing.

"Hey, it's what I do. Expect it." We both laughed as we walked over to where Seth was standing, I was starting to wonder where Lana was now. She said she would come over and she was never late. Maybe something came up. Seth was rubbing his forehead, apparently I had knocked harder than I had intended. Irra cast him a strange look, she wasn't there when he had opened the door so she didn't know what happened.

"Hey guys, where's Lana? She's never late. Did something happen?" I asked, concerned.

"No, nothing happened, she just couldn't make it, she's grounded for a week." Irra informed me. Snickering at something I apparently didn't know.

"What did she do?" I asked, curious. Whenever Lana gets grounded its because of something you would never expect in a million years, last time it was because she clogged her sink with a grape and it flooded the entire bathroom. Only Lana would eat a grape while brushing her teeth.

"Oh, she broke pretty much everything in her entire house." Seth was the one that answered this time. He laughed and so did Irra.

"Wow, how did she do that?!" I asked, my eyes wide in surprise. Lana is weird, but she isn't usually destructive, except that one time with the grape…

"A frog went in through the window and she was chasing it to get it back outside." Irra said. We all fell completely silent for a few seconds. I just blinked at them. Lana must be having the time of her life cleaning that mess up. Especially since her house is so big.

"Well that's Lana for you." I said, Seth, Irra, and I doubled over in laughter. That was the most epic mess up ever. Even for Lana. Which is saying a lot.

Seth and I stopped laughing but Irra was still going. I blinked at her in silence. Seth and I exchanged a look of confusion, it was funny, but it wasn't *that* funny. Then I noticed the monster bag of chips right behind Irra. While she was still laughing I might as well steal one.

I walked over to them slowly and carefully, stepping around Irra who was still having a laughing fit, I opened the bag and stole a chip, I observed it carefully, as I usually do with chips, everyone thinks I'm weird because I look at my chip before I eat it. The second Irra heard the sound of the ripping bag of chips she stopped laughing.

"I SAID I GOT THE FIRST CHIP!" Irra said launching herself at me at full speed, I tried to shove the chip into my mouth but she got to me first, grabbing the chip and ate it herself.

"Blech." She said, "to salty" I snickered at her facial expression; she looked so funny when she made her sour face.

"That's what you get for wanting the first chip," said Seth, using his unfairly long arms to grab the bag from me. He took out a handful of chips and tossed the bag over to the lawn chair farthest from me.

"Hey! What's the big idea? Not cool!" I said stomping over to the bag or chips. I was hungry! I wanted junk food!

"Guys hold on a sec, stop fighting over those stupid chips. I'll be right back." Said Irra as she began walking back towards her house.

Seth and I exchanged a confused glance. I ate about two more chips before Irra returned with a bowl. She snatched the bag from my hands and poured out all the chips into the bowl.

"There, problem solved." Said Irra.

We all sat down on the lawn chairs to talk nonsense as usual. The most important conversation we had ever had that I could remember was that one time we discussed why the rabbit in the Trix commercials, never actually got the stupid Trix. They really should just let him have some; he is completely obsessed with something he has never even tasted. Sad really.

"So, how was it? Did Mr. Jones throw a newspaper at you again Neddy?" Irra asked me. I loved when she used that nickname for me. My real name was to long and sounded like an old lady. Nedaria. God, I hated my name. I snickered remembering the details of my event with Mr. Jones.

"No, a rock." I responded, I watched Seth, and Irra's expressions change into one of disgust and hate. Their eyes widened and I laughed. "Yeah, I know, but he missed."

"So? What if he hadn't?" Irra said, her words made me curious and a little scared, what if he had better aim than he actually did? That would have been a problem.

"I'm getting majorly sick of that old man picking on us, well, mostly you but he always yells at me when I pass by myself, he doesn't disserve us in his neighborhood. He disserves to be surrounded by a bunch of pelicans and seagulls on OldMan Island." Said Seth smirking.

I chucked "Yeah, you're right, should we do something about the old man?" I asked, mostly Seth, considering that Irra was always against pranking, or revenge, she was too nice. The one thing I didn't like about her was that she wouldn't hurt a fly. Usually that's used as an expression, an exaggerated expression, but I really wasn't exaggerating. I was sleeping over at her house once, and a fly was buzzing around and being a little pest. I swatted it and killed it and Irra all but kicked me out of her house, she was so mad about the stupid annoying little fly assassination she gave me an entire lecture on how the fly had feelings, and how I should never kill any living thing. I like nice people, but Irra had to toughen up a bit. At least to the point that she could handle a fly being killed.

So of course it surprised me when she said, "Yeah, why not, lets at least get him to leave you two alone." Seth and I stared at her open-mouthed. Did Irra just agree to help us prank this guy?

I pinched myself just to be sure. "Repeat that please Irra, I don't think I heard right. I thought you said you wanted to help us prank this guy."

"I did." Said Irra smirking slyly; this was so weird in so many ways.

"Well alright what should we do then?" I asked.

"I know what we should do." Seth said.

He broke it down for us, step by step, all I knew was this was going to be fun, very fun, and hopefully it would get Mr. Jones off our backs.

We all set out to the pharmacy, to get one of those stuffed animals that they always have in the window, one of the really big ones that looked really fluffy and awesome. The clerk behind the counter eyed us strangely, usually nobody came in the pharmacy to by the stuffed animals, just the pills and medicine and other nasty tasting stuff.

"That'll be ten dollars please." The clerk informed us. I hated it when people tell you how much something is when there is a sticker on the actual item saying how much it was, I found it extremely irritating. We had also gone to the corner store to by a card.

We went back to Irra's house to start setting up. We addressed the card to Mr. Jones, The card read:

Dear Mr. Jones,

We apologize for all the things that we have done to bother you, please forgive us and accept this gift.

-Seth, and Nedaria

I hated the fact that I had to use my full name but it was much more formal and considering how old people liked that kind of thing…

The big plushy we had bought was a light brown teddy bear, with its arms placed as if the bear was clapping its hands, there was a small amount of space between the two arms of the bear, this is where the real surprise would be hidden. We placed the card on the bear's back; it was kept there with some masking tape. Afterward we got the real weapon. A small, toy, water gun, but it wasn't filled with water, it was actually going to contain mud from a nearby puddle. We filled the water gun with the mud, probably including a bug or two from the puddle. Of course, Seth handled this part, Irra and I were deathly afraid of bugs of any sort, and we really didn't like getting dirty.

"Ok, the mud is in, now I just need a rubber band, to activate the water gun when Mr. Jones touches it. Irra, do you have one around the house somewhere?" Seth asked.

"Yeah, probably, I'll be right back just let me go check the bathroom cabinet." She responded, already turning her back to us and walking out of the room.

"This is going to be sweet." I said, high fiving Seth happily. "He will never bother us again, the guy is a clean freak, although, it'll only be awesome if we don't get killed by Mr. Old Guy himself."

"Neddy, its us against a sixty-year-old man, who do you think can run faster?" Seth said.

"True." I responded.

At that moment, Irra walked back into the room with a rubber band in her hand and something else, something round.

"Gross, what is that smell?" Asked Seth, disgusted by the strengthening odor of raw fish and old garbage.

"That, would be this little thing I call Bob." Irra informed us, holding up the small round object. "Stink bomb, I found it at the entrance of my brothers room, it is only activated when held for a while, so obviously this one already went off." She continued, crinkling her nose.

"Nice!" I said. Seth was smirking; he was probably imagining the expression on Mr. Jones' face when he was sprayed with mud and that disgusting smell.

"So lets get going then!" Irra said, as she placed the stink bomb behind the water gun in between the bear's arms.

We all laughed and came up with funny outcomes to how we thought Mr. Jones would react to his little surprise while we walked over to his house. Seth and I hid behind a tree in front of his yard, knowing that he would never take the bear if he saw me or Seth deliver it to his yard. Mr. Jones was in his front yard as usual. Irra said nothing as she stepped up and placed the bear on his lawn.

Irra turned her back and walked back toward us.

"What the…" Mr. Jones said, as he approached the bear.

He read the card and stared at the bear for a few seconds before picking it up. He touched the water gun slightly, triggering it to start spraying, and because the stink bomb was so close to the water gun, that went off too.

"STUPID KIDS! I HATE THEM SO MUCH!" Mr. Jones stomped toward where we were hiding and Seth jumped out from behind the tree and taunted Mr. Jones. Seth broke into a run yelling something about how slow Mr. Jones was.

Mr. Jones stared after Seth and turned his attention toward me. I broke into a run as well, going quickly after Seth and escaping the wrath of Mr. Jones. I caught up to Seth pretty fast, we were both laughing when Irra caught up to us. I looked back to see if Mr. Jones was still chasing us. He was, but he gave up when a small Chihuahua came out of nowhere and started chasing him.

I laughed so hard, along with Seth and Irra that I almost lost my footing.

"That was fun." I said, still laughing.

"You think?" said Seth and Irra at the exact same time. "Jinx!" They said again "I said it first" They continued. All I could do was laugh.

Best. Day. Ever.

CHAPTER 12

Rich Kids

Ludy Ambroise
8th grade

One morning Angelie and her friends were out shopping to for outfits to wear to her other friend's birthday party. After three hours of shopping Angelie and her friend Jessica got really hungry. At first they were going to burger king but Jessica had suggested to Angelie that they go to the restaurant they both enjoy. Little did Angelie know that her twin whom she didn't know of because her parents did not want to tell her was busy getting into trouble. When she and her sister were young their house caught on fire and they found Angelie but not Vanessa they were searching for years to find her but didn't. The day of the fire a kind lady gave her to an orphanage but the orphanage had changed her name to Samantha Rodriguez even though her name was Vanessa Lopez. This was a life changing experience for her family because Vanessa was pronounced dead. Vanessa was so tired of the orphanage that she ran away which was normal but this time she left before lunch and she was so hungry. Vanessa decided to go to the restaurant to go beg for money to buy food. As she turns around she spots the officer who always catches her and brings her back to the orphanage so she runs away but bumps into Angelie. Angelie was so surprised when she saw Vanessa that everything in her mind went blank. To make matters worse her father walked in and wasn't really happy because he saw the credit card she did a lot of damage in three hours. Angelie's dad had plans to walk in and scream at her but when he saw Vanessa he was happy, surprised, and shocked. Jessica in shock drops her purse. Angelie finally got the courage to speak "OMG who are you? Where did you come from? Why do look like me? Vanessa says "Sorry sir but why does your daughter look like me? Angelie's dad says "call me Mr. Lopez ok I'm at most shock as well". Mr. Lopez says "lets run go to the hospital and run some DNA test". Angelie says "you still didn't answer my question". Vanessa responds "well I'm Samantha Rodriguez and well I'm not sure I was put in an orphanage as a child and I'm also not sure why I look like you". Angelie says "well I'm Angelie Lopez". Angelie also said "when you birthday and what year are you born? Vanessa replies and says "June 1st 1993 I'm turning sixteen". That's my birthday and I'm turning sixteen. Mr. Lopez says girls lets go to the hospital". When they arrive at the hospital at the hospital they get tested and the girls are related as twins that was an even bigger shock. Angelie's parents told the girls what happened when they were young and Angelie was mad at her father. Angelie was not mad because she had a sister she was mad that it now that they decide to tell her that she wasn't an only child. Angelie also felt as if she could trust her parents anymore and she wondered if her parents kept anything away else away from her. What had just realized that if she and Vanessa had never met each other they would have never known that they were related. Vanessa thought wow now I have a family now but sadly I don't think they like me because Angelie is furious at her parents this would have never happened if she had never left the orphanage. Vanessa quickly tries to escape but at the time the door bell had rang and there goes the officer that always catchers her but this time he came for something else. Officer says "have you seen a girl about 5 foot tall and 4 inches (shows Mrs. Lopez a picture of the girl Vanessa) and look like this. Mrs. Lopez says "yeah that look like my daughters (shows the officer her daughters) you see. Officer said astonished "what impossible there was only one Samantha Rodriguez".

Mrs. Lopez told the officer what had happened when they were younger and he was in shock. Officer says "what are going to about it"? Mrs. Lopez responds "I'm not sure what do you do in a situation like this"? Officer says "I'm not sure either". Mrs. Lopez says "kids what think about this"? Kids answer "this is complicated". Mr. Lopez says "why don't we call the friends that helped us search for Vanessa and ask them. Mrs. Lopez says "good idea nick I'm going to start calling". Mr. Lopez says "good honey I'll make dinner". Angelie says "Vanessa and I will go chat in the living room". Angelie says "so how was life in the orphanage"? Vanessa replies "its terrible mean the foods great the people are okay but I and three other people are left and they were about to send us to another orphanage because the one were in is closing down that's why I ran away". Angelie says "wow I didn't know life was this hard". Vanessa says "are you kind of mad because I bump into you and you know the rest of what happened"? Angelie says "know not really I'm kind of happy because lately I've been feeling kind of lonely". Vanessa says "now I know how it feels to have a family and it feels good. Mr. Lopez says "dinners ready". Vanessa says "oh good I'm hungry". Angelie says "me too". Suddenly Mrs. Lopez says "we need to go to court tomorrow bright and early". The next day they arrive at the court house they walk in the same time the judge did the judge said "this case is familiar". Mrs. Lopez said "isn't this the judge we had the first time". Mr. Lopez said "yeah I think so". In an hour Vanessa was pronounced alive and aloud to live with her family and they lived peacefully.

The End

CHAPTER 13

Roaming

Brandon Perez

On a bright sunny day Michael is walk out of his house yawning and tired. He walked down the block and says hi to a little old lady. Michael was 20 years old and was 5 ft 11 inches, with no job and was waiting to go to a business school. So that he can become a stock broker. He lives in one bedroom house in the Bronx. Walking down the block without a care in the world, going where ever life takes him.

"Yo Michael" a man screams as he runs up to him. "What" Michael yelled back?

"Gang meeting" the guy says.

"Man right now, why now Jackie "we got a bust on a rich man, down the block from the bank" Jackie told Michael.

"Alright lets go" Michael responded.

We walked to an alley; we can see garbage cans all over the place. Then an alley cat ran in front of us and jumped in a garbage can. Then a crowd of people appeared out of the shadows.

"Good everyone" someone yelled out of the darkness, a man appeared with a black bat in his hand. A big guy with a chin in his hand appears too.

"Yo Michael, we got a hit on the block down from the bank" The man with the bat said.

"We have a long time to attack, so will plan it" the man suggested.

"Ok Alex we do have time, so what time person we are dealing with" Jackie said.

"Oh we have rich white man, yo know the ones that red in the face" Alex says.

"Alright it's time to gets some money" Alex says.

The gang moved out and went down the block from the bank there stood a man standing up with nice clothes on. He walked down the block and fall right into a tarp. Alex popped out of corner of an alley screaming "help, help"!!!!

The rich man ran into the alley and everyone swarm around him and then Alex said any last words. The rich man said "yeah FBI you're all under arrest".

Ones he said that everyone started running, Police stormed into the alley. We were died I jumped over a garbage can ran into a basement door. With me Jackie and Alex, and a couple of gang members, we stormed up some stairs into the lobby of the building and ran out of the building. The gang spilt up ones we hit the street and I went into another alley with Jackie. "That was close" I said to Jackie. I walked away and left to my house.

"yeah that was close" Michael said.

"But tomorrow I will roam again" Michael.

CHAPTER 14

Charles the Cannibal

The workers of the "Abridged Asylum" were all startled to the sight of the two large, metal doors that withstood them from the outside world slammed open. Charles Benoviet was escorted into the asylum by nine federal officers each armed with semi-automatic rifles and tazzers each loaded at 1600 watts. Charles was wheeled into the asylum on a long table, which looked like a stretcher, standing vertically upright. The permanent record that stated everything that Charles has done in the past which has been noticed as illegal was placed into the hands of the head manager of the asylum. The officer watched as the manager's eyes read over the large printed name on the front of the folder (Charles Benoviet). The manager tucked the vanilla colored folder behind his back and shook hands with the officer. Charles watched the big, metal doors spring open again and the nine agents all stepped outside leaving Charles with the workers of the "Abridged Asylum". As the two doors were slowly shut, the head officer of the eight others (Mr. Richard Wright) took one glance back at Charles. Charles looked up toward Mr. Richard Wright and through the small crack of the door as it was finally about to close, Mr. Richard Wright noticed a large smirk that had come across Charles' face. The two doors slammed tight and were locked down by two workers. As this happened, a deep sense of fear came across Mr. Richard Wright's body, but he swallowed hard an walked away to the chopper that brought them to the Island that the "Abridged Asylum" was laid upon. Inside the asylum, Charles was thinking quickly of a plan to escape. He noticed how each and every worker was only armed with low powered tazzers. He quickly and easily hatched a plan that will get him out of the asylum in no time. Three workers walked over to Charles

CHAPTER 15

Zodiac Adventure

Deandra Kellman

My, Oh my! I'm getting kind 'a board on this planet! I should seek some adventure! I just can't stand still! I am a Sagittarius anyway. Chose ruler from the God King Jupiter! I'll shall go off and call this Zodiac adventure! This could help me study find new knowledge. I could also find the famous rulers of these planet's or maybe even stars! I'll go off to the Sun. I have to study the creatures! I must meet the famous ruler. King Leo!

"King Sagittarius" "We have prepared for your Adventure of wisdom and knowledge" "you should know that King Leo of the Sun is a very fierce type" "you might encounter some … difficulties" Hum? I Interesting. King Leo, is he a fire type? "Yes your majesty" "But dose it not matter rather or not the King is a fire, earth, water, or air type?" Yes. You have a lot to learn if you would like to handle things. "I'm very sorry your majesty" We'll I'll prepare for my lift off! If there anything I should change into, it should be a Phoenix. It will be able to with stand the heat of the Sun.

The Sun is hotter than I thought it would be. It's expanding my wings and my flames! It is toasty here! How dose king Leo and his subject's survive here!? I should be near the city of the Sun {Sun Ruby] in right about now……thump!!! WHAT IN THE MILKYWAY IS THIS!!!!!! Who installed an invisible shield here [inside the shield] Hum hum! Hum! "Halt their" "Who are you" "and what's the noise" I'm King Sagittarius and as you see I'm angry about THIS SHIELD! "Where very sorry as much as you would like to move the shield King Leo made this to cool us down in here and kept us from the fire storms" Oh my bad. I'm for that."Any who, we are humble for you to be at this hot or cold town of ours" "Our King, King Leo will be surprise for your visit" "Please we do ask you not to flirt with thy majesties wife queen Sarfiti" "King Leo has a thing for that" "Also…." Enough I know how I should act and that you should be… "Hem" "King Sagittarius isn't it" Yes. "Hi I'm Queen Sarfiti" "King Leo's wife" How do you do thy queen. "Very welcomed to see you here" "Shall we" "My Oh my" "Who interrupts me in my mourning nap!?" One that is awakens in the royal chamber of warmth. "My Oh my" We didn't expect you to be here at our glorious city Sun Ruby". It is my honor to meet such a famous king on this glorious star. Well your planet isn't that bad just 'orbit's around me" What did you say. :("What being king of just a planet isn't that bad" What and you think just because you live on our solar star that you are as glorious as it! "Now what is that suppose to mean!" "You just think that you are greater than everybody else because you are on a star!!!" "There's many reason's of me being great and you plain" WHAT!!!!!!!! YOU Insolent KING!!! ARG!!! "So you want to spit fire then go ahead!!!!" It'll be my pleasure! Zoush boom

"WHAT IS GOING ON!!!!!!!!!!!!!!!!!!!!!!!" "You are kings for crying out loud!" Fire sign's as well you shouldn't be fighting" "Please your king's" "For anything at all is that king Leo will go out with Sagittarius on the journey. Do you agree?" We agree" because you are on a star!!!" "There's many reason's of me being great and you plain" WHAT!!!!!!!! YOU INSILTE KING!!! ARG!!! "So you want to spit fire then go ahead!!!!" It'll be my pleasure! Zoush boom "WHAT IS GOING ON!!!!!!!!!!!!!!!!!!!!!!!" "You are kings for crying out loud!" Fire sign's as well you shouldn't be fighting" "Please you are king's" For anything at all is that king Leo will go out with Sagittarius on the journey. "Well, I guess I went a little too far" "It's up to the centaur!" Well, you are kind 'a annoying, but the company I won't mind. So yes I guess. "Bye!" "Be kind to each other!" We will! "So where do we go next?" We will be going to Mars. I hear that the ruler is also a fire sign. They say she's very beautiful. "Well I'm with you to the end"